Grandfather Speaks

Books by Bob Anderson

Sarge, What Now?
Anderson Rules

TAC Leader Series
#1 What Honor Requires
#2 Night Hawks
#3 Retribution

Books by Jerry Ahern, Sharon Ahern and Bob Anderson

The Survivalist Series
#30 The Inheritors of the Earth
#31 Earth Shine
#32 The Quisling Covenant

The Rourke Chronicles
#1 Everyman

Short Stories
Shades of Love
Once Upon a Time
Light Dreams

For more exciting
Books, eBooks, Audiobooks and more visit us at
www.speakingvolumes.us

Grandfather Speaks

Bob Anderson

SPEAKING VOLUMES, LLC
NAPLES, FLORIDA
2015

Grandfather Speaks

Copyright © 2012 by Bob Anderson

Cover photo of eagle by Paul Gregg.
Editing assistance provided by Pamela Anderson and Paul
Gregg.

ISBN 978-1-62815-217-3

To my Comanche blood brother,
Donnie Three Wolves Morgan.

To "all of my Chiefs and all of my Indians,"
and to all of the Cowboys and Outlaws.

To Mom, Dad, Roger, John, Shelley
and to the best grandkids a
Paw Paw could have—Sarah, Rachel,
Kayleigh, Josh and Seth.

To my wife, Pam, who lives it with me.

On 1 July 2000, I was promoted to the rank of Chief Master Sergeant in the United States Air Force Reserve. That event allowed for many wonderful things to follow.

This rank, E-9, is the highest rank an enlisted member can attain. I have been told that less than one percent of the enlisted force achieves it. When the rank was created in the 1950s, a decision was made to use the Native American Chief as the symbol of this rank.

I was particularly honored by this promotion because my paternal grandmother, Alma "Mom" Anderson, was French and Indian. Her maiden name was DeShazier and she was part Cherokee.

I had always been intrigued by the fact that I was part Indian (the term Native American had not yet come into play when I was a child). Crazy Horse, Sitting Bull, Red Cloud and Cochise were as much my heroes as Roy Rogers and the Lone Ranger.

When I became a "Chief," it allowed me to exercise my heritage. I obtained a feathered war bonnet, something I had wanted since I was a child. I obtained some pipestone and carved a pipe. I had been making dream catchers for several years and continued.

I began to harvest birds that had been killed along the roadways for their feathers. This involved sprinkling tobacco in the four directions before picking them up. I would place the birds in a plastic bag and when I returned home, harvest their feathers. This was not always a pleasant or sanitary process, as you can imagine.

One of the problems was after short periods of decomposition the feathers would pull out, but they would retain their cuticle. This is the sheath from which the feather grows. Several times this cuticle would be hard and difficult to cut off, even with a sharp knife.

One day, after a particularly difficult session, I grabbed the cuticle of one feather between my index finger and my thumb nail and jerked. It came right off. At that moment I realized I had "relearned" something my ancestors had known for years, even centuries.

Maybe it was coincidence. Maybe it was a race memory; I don't know, but it worked.

Another day, I noticed that I had cut my finger. It was not a serious cut, but I knew I had received it because I had disregarded something important. My father had taught me to "Never cut toward you." I imagined how many times that statement had been spoken throughout the course of time, in how many languages, in how many lands.

In that moment a flood of "truths" washed over me. Like, "Never cut toward yourself, always cut away from you." As I pondered this concept, I had to wonder. How many times have untold numbers of fathers, uncles or older brothers spoken those words to a young man? How many untold mothers, aunts or older sisters have spoken those words to young women?

The sheer number of times that phrase has been spoken in a multitude of languages must make it one of the most repeated phrases in human history.

It reminded me of something I discovered almost thirty years ago, "All thoughts that can be thought, have been thought, I think." Our task in learning is not to try to come up with new ideas, as much as it is to "relearn" what we already know.

From these simple incidents grew the realization that "Old truths are simple truths and they are just as relevant today as they were the first time they were spoken."

When I decided to write *Grandfather Speaks,* I tackled it the same way I have with other books I've written. However, *Grandfather* had other ideas. As I wrote, I became aware that my thoughts had taken on a different pattern, a different beat and a new rhythm.

I began to rewrite what I had written according to these new patterns, this new way of thinking and speaking. I don't know about other authors but when I write, I hear the words before they are written. As I wrote, Bob Anderson was replaced by G*randfather.* HE was telling the stories, I was just writing them down. I didn't complain because what he had to say I felt was much better than what I had to say. He spoke to me as though we were sitting around a campfire. He spoke to me as my ancestors told their stories, their verbal history.

Several times we argued because of words he used that I realized my audience would not understand. Several times I could feel his resentment that I was so slow in writing this.

Yet, like all good grandfathers, his reproaches were gentle and designed to move me forward as I wrote his stories.

The more I wrote the more real he became. I could smell the smoke of the campfire, I could hear the wolves in the distance, and I could feel his presence. I saw him as he sat there in buckskin shirt and breeches with his simple moccasins.

His hair was past his shoulders, marbled with gray and black. His face wrinkled as only sun tanned skin will wrinkle. His voice was soft but firm and had no tremble associated with age.

His eyes were clear but I knew he was not seeing what I was seeing. He was seeing what had been and what was to come. We talked and I asked him questions that he never seemed to quite answer. Instead he told stories and asked me questions.

Those were where my answers were; he was just guiding me to them. He was in no hurry to satisfy my curiosity.

Truth is truth, he would say. ***You want answers to all questions and you have not yet asked the right questions. You young people are all alike—white, red. No difference.***

To be called a young person the month before my sixtieth birthday was both flattering and humbling. This man knew great age. He had seen many things and could see many more that had not yet happened.

I realized he was what I had looked for in much of my wanderings and many of my writings. Here was a sage, available for my questions.

Here was history as it had happened. Here was the future, if I was smart enough to listen.

I realized he never told me his name. I called him *Grandfather* from the moment I became aware of him and that is what I will always think of him as—*Grandfather.*

So in the language of my Cherokee brothers, "O si yo," hello, I hope you enjoy *Grandfather Speaks.*

Chapter One

The night was still and clear. Above my head I could see every star God had ever made. I had no idea how I got here. One minute I was typing at my computer and the next minute I was here; I had no idea where "here" was, but it sure was not Houston, Texas.

I turned 360 degrees and could not see any glow on any horizon that said I was close to a large town. I watched and saw several shooting stars but no lights from any aircraft. There was a nip in the air and I wasn't dressed for it. As I walked, I could smell a wood fire burning and I reasoned it was behind a small hill.

I thought it was hunters or campers; they at least could tell me where I was, so I started around the hill. I called out, "Hello the camp."

A voice came out of the darkness, ***Come sit with me. We will make talk, we will make smoke. There is much to learn.***

I rounded the small hill but it was not hunters waiting on me. There was a fire, but it was a campfire, a small campfire. The sticks and branches were stacked into a pyramid and I noticed one had a curious knot that reminded me of a face looking back from the fire.

Sitting on a log next to the fire was an old man. No, that is not accurate. This was an ancient Indian. I apologize for my political incorrectness but I grew up before the term Native American was popular.

So here I was having no idea where that was, but sharing space and time with an ancient Native American.

He wore a buckskin shirt and breeches with moccasins. He had a simple headband also of buckskin. His shirt was laced and had natural dyes that been applied in patterns. He sat on a blanket on the log and pointed to another log across the fire and facing him.

He reminded me of the great Native American character actor of the 1980's, Chief Dan George. He said, **Come, sit with me. We will make talk, we will make smoke. There is much to learn.**

"Thanks Grandfather, but I really need some answers. I don't know where I am," I said.

You are here, with me, he replied.

"I have no idea of how I got here."

We came together you and I; for here is where we are supposed to be.

"I have no idea why I am here," I responded.

To talk, to make smoke, to learn.

"Talk about what, what are we smoking and what is there to learn?"

Talk about all things, smoke the pipe and there is everything to learn. Sit.

I gave up and sat down on a log, wrapping a blanket around my shoulders to warm up.

Do you have paper? he asked.

I realized I had a pen and pad in my hands that hadn't been there a moment ago. He saw them and did not wait for an answer.

Good, I'll talk, you write. I know you will change my words that aren't acceptable, but do not change the messages.

I nodded and he began to talk. I began to write.

In the beginning, he said, *we are all fresh clay that is waiting to be molded. Some of that clay is light colored, some darker colored in varying shades. No matter, it is all clay.*

The most important thing to recognize is that we SHALL BE molded. We shall be molded by activity or we shall settle due to inactivity. In the daily aspects of living, lessons are taught.

Just as in the training of young warriors or white children in classroom at school, some of these lessons are learned, some misinterpreted and some are ignored all together.

Long before there were formal schools with classrooms and desks and black boards, learning still occurred.

In those days learning was done by watching and doing and being shown what was wrong with what was done. We learned by doing. We were taught 'best practices' and the 'right way' to do things.

These had been learned over the years by doing. Many of these life skills had been passed down from father to son and mother to daughter for generations.

"From a cultural anthropological standpoint," I said, "we learned what we needed to survive, then we learned what we needed to prosper, then we learned what we wanted to learn."

I know not the cultural antelope, he said. ***Our life was simpler then. We were more in touch with nature and we had less to clutter our minds.***

I said, "But you have to admit, we have greater conveniences today."

All of a sudden his appearance shifted. When I had first met him he looked like Chief Dan George. Now his visage was that of Iron Eyes Cody, the famous Native American with a tear running down his cheek in commercials talking about the environment.

But at what cost? he said.

However he looked, I thought, "He is right!" Twenty years ago, only a small number of people had cell phones. Now they are considered a necessary commodity. Twenty years ago, computers were the size of stereo cabinets, now they fit in your hand.

Twenty years ago, people could actually leave the job at work. It is now almost impossible to escape from the job. What has always been a scary thought for me is that one day these will be the "good ol' days" for someone else.

As though he could read my mind, he said, *That is the way of things, however. It is relative. What occurs to ME has significance. What happens to ME is important. What happens NOW is relevant.*

What has already happened is what you whites call history and therefore not as important.

This is in direct conflict to the learning that took place around our campfires. We told our stories and, in the telling, those stories came alive.

In that way, our children met their ancestors and because they heard their words and their stories, they became real. Now we read books, he snorted.

How can a man become real when he lives in a book? How can a story be told in silence? Our way was better. Now, it is more important to have the written languages.

Today, anyone can buy a book but still not everyone can read. All people, except those that the Great Spirit has taken, have ears to hear. Not all people can read what is written.

Yet, you call this progress. I think not. Our stories were truth.

Chapter Two

He continued as he puffed on a pipe. It had a long wooden stem and was decorated with horse hair, feathers and carvings. The stem was carved from a red stone; from my studies I knew this was a calumet or what the white man called a peace pipe.

He took another puff before saying, *Much of what I have read in books is the white man's history. I know his history has lied about my people, why then do I believe anything in his books?*

Somewhat confused, I said, "But you have asked me to write what you say down so I can use it in my books."

No! I told you to write it down so you will remember when you leave here. Words are like sparrows the children catch and play with; some escape, some die and some are released. In any event, what happens to them happens and we cannot control that.

"That's not true," I said. "We caught them in the first place; at that moment we became responsible for them. It is our job to be responsible for those birds or, in this case, the words."

He smiled, **You are so young. Do you think that because a child builds a trap that it is inevitable the bird will land in it? The child wants to catch a bird. The bird must allow himself to be caught. Who then is responsible?**

I said, "But after the catch is made..."

The bird might escape, that is his responsibility. The bird might die. Animals can will themselves to death, for that may be their only escape. Who is responsible?

The child may have a soft heart and wish to care for the bird. The bird may wish to visit for a time with man. After a while the spirit of the bird speaks to the spirit of the child and says, 'I must go now' and the child decides to release the bird.

Who is responsible? It is the same with words.

Who is responsible? My tongue is different from your tongue, but I have learned your tongue. What do you know of mine?

"Very little, I admit. I can say hello and thank you in your tongue; that is all I know right now."

He thought for a moment and puffed the pipe before saying, ***Those are good words to know. In fact, I think they are some of the best words to know. In saying O si yo, you greet a stranger or meet a friend again. This is good. With Wa Do, you say thanks for what others have done for you. This is good.***

"I deal in words," I said. "I want them to be accurate. I want them to tell a story the right way..."

He interrupted, ***It is not you that can make that decision. It is the words that make that decision. You may write them down and, in that writing, you may be correct and truthful. But the words will speak to different people in different ways.***

If your words are translated from your tongue into mine, they will change. You people have words for things my people do not speak of. We have words for things your people do not dream of.

How then can you speak of words that do not exist? You cannot. You must find something similar that another can use to compare.

Your people have the word locomotive, my people did not. We had iron and we had horse, so my people called the locomotive the iron horse, he explained.

The words mean different things to different people but they describe the same thing. Now, whose responsibility is that? Is it the words' responsibility? No, others.

"Okay," I said, realizing that his mind was made up and discussion would not change his position. "But I want my readers to hear my story and understand it."

This is good but it is also silly. That is a white man's wish. To control the other man, so he hears what you wish him to. He needs to understand your message. I think he has his own hearing. He has his own messages. Why does he need yours?

Chapter Three

I bristled, "Because I have something important to say with my books. I want him to learn from them, to be better because of them."

Grandfather chuckled. **What do you have to say that has not been said before? Nothing. What do you think that has not been thought before? Nothing.**

The owl, wisest of all beasts, told me one night, "All thoughts that can be thought, have been thought, I think."

I sat quietly thinking about this; he leaned over the fire to hand me the pipe. Without thinking, I took it and puffed. We sat for a long time saying nothing as I pondered the words of the owl. Finally, I said, "Did the owl really talk to you?"

My son, all animals speak. It is man's responsibility to hear. In the old days, we spoke the same language. That was before man changed. Some of us still listen and can hear.

I sat quietly again and smoked the pipe. I examined the pipe and asked, "Did you make this?" He nodded. I asked, "What is the stone the bowl is made from?"

Your people call it Catlinite after a white man that came through our nations long ago, he said. *This man was called George Catlin, he made pictures of our peoples and our way of life.*

He walked among us with open arms and empty hands in peace and accepted us as people. My people call the stone pipe-stone.

True pipestone comes from a quarry near a town in Minnesota. It too is called Pipestone. It is a reddish rock that when quarried is soft and easily worked with hand tools, even a knife.

When exposed to air it becomes harder. This rock is considered sacred to the tribes that use it.

The red color is believed by some to be the blood of our ancestors. The making of a pipe, using only hand tools, is a signifi-cant sacred event.

"Where did you get yours?" I asked.

I traded for a block of pipestone from Minnesota and traced a traditional design.

With a knife and some tools I set out to fashion this pipe.

It is my personal pipe. I roughed out the shape of the bowl and the base the bowl sits on. I cut the holes for the bowl and stem.

Then I let the stone tell me what was inside of it. As time allowed, I sat with the bowl and shaped it with the files. Slowly, a set of wings appeared around the front of the base of the bowl; next a star and finally a diamond.

I carved, sanded, and polished for many days before I was satisfied the bowl had shown itself to me.

With the soft red color it looks like a mini constellation that dropped from the sky and turned to stone. Can you see the white stars in it?

I nodded.

I even saved the dust created by the carving. I have given it to several friends in small pouches. I tell them it is magic dust, and I sense that there is a magic in this stone.

I felt a great sense of serenity and peace while I worked on it. Nothing I have ever worked on with my hands filled me with such a sense of accomplishment and purpose. Then I started on the stem. I looked for sumac.

"What is that?"

It is a woody shrub that has a soft center and is a favorite of my people for pipe stems.

Unfortunately, there was no sumac where I was at the time. I went through several frustrating attempts at drilling a hole through a branch, from one end to the other.

Finally, I was successful. After tying several feathers and carving designs in the stem, I assembled the pipe.

"It is beautiful."

He smiled and said, **Wa do.**

"Grandfather," I asked again. "Why am I here?"

To learn my son.

"Grandfather, where am I; how did I get here?"

15

You are where you are, he said. *You came seeking me. I am here. It is good, yet it is also the way of things that many questions have no answers. None, that is, that we will understand while we walk the prairie. One day when we sit at the big campfire with the Great Spirit, we will know all things.*

That is enough for now, sleep. We will talk again.

Chapter Four

I slept. In my dreams, Grandfather came to me and told me the story of a Sioux legend he called The Gift of the Peace Pipe.[1]

Two young men were out strolling one night talking of love affairs. They passed around a hill and came to a little ravine or coulee. Suddenly they saw coming up from the ravine a beautiful woman. She was painted and her dress was of the very finest material.

"What a beautiful girl!" said one of the young men.

"Already I love her. I will steal her and make her my wife."

"No," said the other. "Don't harm her. She may be holy."

The young woman approached and held out a pipe which she first offered to the sky, then to the earth and then advanced, holding it out in her extended hands.

"I know what you young men have been saying; one of you is good; the other is wicked," she said.

She laid down the pipe on the ground and at once became a buffalo cow. The cow pawed the ground, stuck her tail straight out behind her and then lifted the pipe from the ground again in her hoofs; immediately she became a young woman again.

"I am come to give you this gift," she said. "It is the peace pipe. Hereafter all treaties and ceremonies shall be performed after smoking it. It shall bring peaceful thoughts into your minds. You shall offer it to the Great Mystery and to mother earth."

The two young men ran to the village and told what they had seen and heard. All the village came out where the young woman was.

She repeated to them what she had already told the young men and added, "When you set free the ghost, you must have a white buffalo cow skin."

She gave the pipe to the medicine men of the village, turned again to a buffalo cow and fled away to the land of buffaloes.

Chapter Five

When I awoke I was back in Houston, TX. I thought to myself, "Damn, what a dream." The strangest thing was this was not like other dreams I had. Generally, if you remember a dream at all, it is only for a short time after you wake up, then the dream drifts away.

Not this one; throughout the day I kept remembering more from the dream.

I remembered what Grandfather had said about books. I knew the history of books; I used to work as a printer. Before Johann Gutenberg made the first printing press, all books were transcribed by hand and they were very expensive.

When moveable type was created, the printing press became an industrial revolution of its own. Books could now be made for far less money and with far less effort.

For the first time in history, there was something that everyone could read—not just the rich, not just the clergy. The next step was to increase the number of people that could read.

Literature was reborn, but it was not all roses as the poet says.

In Mexico, the Mayans wrote wooden books called codicils. These were promptly destroyed during the Christianization of the "barbarian tribes." These were the same "barbarian tribes" that had created a culture that rivaled anything in Europe or Egypt. Priests tasked with civilizing a new world burned almost the entire history of that world.

Today, books and the written language are taken for granted. Books are written and printed in a volume incomprehensible just fifty years ago.

Written communication is suffering now that email and texting have become a fact. Written communication is now undergoing a shorthand process that increases the speed of communication, as the electronic technology increases the distance over which we can communicate.

This is the advantage of technology. I then remembered something Grandfather had said. ***As a thing becomes easier to accomplish, it loses its value. At the start of all things,*** we struggle to learn a new technique, master a new skill or accomplish a new task.

For a while it occupies the forefront of our thoughts and energies. Eventually, we master the task and suddenly it becomes easy.

At that moment the task, technique or skill begins to lose value. It is in the pursuit of a goal that man is happiest, not in the having.

What we have—we no longer seek.

That is why the Great Spirit allowed us to lose our way and become separated from him. We only value what we search for.

Chapter Six

For many years I have suspected that God set us up. We had paradise and everything that man could ever want in that Garden. The world was filled with peace and beauty but God had given man free will. Understanding that is sort of like when my grandkids would come over when they were little.

Paw Paw Bob (that's me), will say, "Why don't y'all go outside and play? I have cleaned up the yard and taken everything out of it that can hurt you. Go have fun but don't get on the fence. The fence can hurt you and if you diso- bey, Paw Paw will have to spank you."

Okay parents and grandparents, what do you think will happen next?

Exactly. As soon as the door closes, some of the grandkids will go out into the yard and begin playing. But I have one that will go climb on the fence, who then suckers her cousin in and she climbs on board also.

Two others will begin telling them, "You bet- ter get off of that," and the last one is headed in to find me.

We are all children in spirit. We do not grow up, we grow older. We get bigger, stronger, sometimes smarter and certainly more skilled. Some, like me, even return to their first haircut but we all remain children in His sight.

We need to play and we need to find our limits, our boundaries. We push our limitations. We strive to attain the unattainable.

The ongoing and never-ending search for what we, as people, threw away in the Garden of Eden has been the salvation of man. It is not the having that is important; it is the seeking.

In the having you can only examine what is there. In the seeking, you can experience all that could be, can be, might be, should be and ought to be. Which is the greater treasure; having paradise or seeking it?

I remembered also what Grandfather said about words, particularly those lost in translation from one language to another. My studies had shown that as white America began to civilize the Native American, this often happened in schools run by whites.

The children of Native Americans were sent or brought to these schools. They were dressed like white children and, in most cases, forbidden to speak their native tongue.

They were required to speak in English, read in English and learn in English. Remember that in the late 1800s, America was fully involved in the Industrial Revolution and technology was progressing at a rate that would not be equaled again until decades after the turn of the century.

Yet here were children that had come from a culture that had little, if any, technology.

Their families were hunter-gathers or farmers.

It was not long ago that their implements had been stone and bone. It wasn't until the white man came to the new world that the Native Americans even had horses. Most tribes did not have the wheel.

Movement of possessions and supplies was done on the backs of people or dogs or pulled on travois behind the people and dogs.

After the white man started landing in the new world, horses were traded by the whites or, most often, they escaped or were stolen by Indians.

Those who escaped began roaming wild and reverted to a feral state eventually forming great herds. Native Americans hunted and tamed the descendants of these horses.

When Cortez landed in the New World in 1521, the Aztecs (the predominant aborigine nation in what is now called Mexico) had never seen a man on horseback and thought they were a monster—part man and part animal.

Scarcely 300 years later, the Plains Indians developed into the most effective light cavalry since the Mongol hordes of Genghis Khan.

As I pondered these thoughts, I wondered when, and if, I would speak with Grandfather again.

Chapter Seven

I awoke with a start; yet, I was not awake.

It was night and the sky was still and clear—again. I could see the stars clearly as I had before. Again, I had no idea how I got here. One minute I was typing on my computer and the next minute I was here—again.

As I walked, I could smell the campfire's smoke and see its soft glow. I called out, "Hello the camp."

A voice came out of the darkness, **Come, sit with me. We will make talk, we will make smoke. There is much to learn.**

I approached and he was sitting there again. He sat on the same blanket on the same log and pointed again to the other log across the fire and facing him.

He said, **Come, sit with me. We will make talk, we will make smoke. There is much to learn.**

I took my place across the fire from him and said, "Grandfather, it is good to see you again. I did not know when, or if, I would be able to visit with you again."

He smiled and said, **It is good to see you my son, but you need not worry or think of such things. You will come when you are ready to come.**

"But I had no thought of coming, it just happened."

He smiled, saying, **It is the way of things that they will happen when they are supposed to and not when we want them to. What do you wish to discuss this evening?**

I looked at the fire and realized it was the same fire I had seen last time. I don't mean the flames; all flames are alike. I mean the wood. I recognized the same stick with a knot that looked like a face peering out of the fire.

"My first question is, why has this wood not burned up? Those are the same sticks that were burning on my last visit. I recognize that piece with the knot on the side. Yet it is unburned; how can that be?"

Grandfather smiled and said, **Why, it is magic of course.**

I thought for a moment and asked, "Grandfather, what is magic?"

All that we do not understand is magic.

27

"But is magic real? And if so, how does it work?"

There are things of man that we understand. The ways of the Great Spirit are not for us to know. They simply are and that is enough and as it should be.

That was not the answer I wanted. I asked, "But if magic is real, why can't we use it to help make things better?"

Grandfather reached into the fire and pulled out a burning twig. He asked, **What then is 'better?' How is it you believe that you know a better way than the Great Spirit?**

"But look at our world," I said. "We have war and crime. People suffer every day needlessly. People, good people, die. We treat each other like animals; it is not a good world. If I could use magic, I could change all of that."

He smiled as he put the burning twig to the bowl of his pipe. When he had it going the way he wanted, he held up the twig, waved it in the air and it disappeared.

"How did you do that?" I shouted.

Do what?

"The twig; how did you make it disappear?"

He smiled and said, **Magic.** **You do not understand that you already have all of the magic any man may possess. It is because you see what is wrong with the world that you think it needs changing. You do not understand the Great Spirit's plan.**

"Okay, you say I already have magic. You say I don't understand. Explain it to me."

I shall try. If you want to hunt the deer, you must think like a deer. Too often, man will seek a goal with no more understanding of that goal than a gopher has.

Like the magpie, we see something shiny and we want it. We don't know why we want it, we just do. It is much like the dog chasing the car. What would he do if he caught it?

Man is like the dog and the magpie. We collect shiny things that have no meaning. We pursue that which we cannot catch and, if we did, we would have no use of it.

People talk of seeking success and happiness. Yet, they do not study success or happiness. They only see that it is shiny or that it is in motion and they launch off in

pursuit of it. You must become what you hunt.

You must value what you seek and understand what it values. You will not find an eagle in a cave. You will not find a deer in the top of a tree.

To be successful, you must determine what success is for you. For some, they believe that it is money. For others, they think it is power.

For others, they think it is control. When they attain what they have spent a lifetime pursuing, they realize they are not successful.

Chapter Eight

They are not fulfilled and so their seeking begins again. It is like marriage. Only the wolf and the hawk mate for life.

"Tell me what you mean," I said.

Many men and more women marry and find one day that they are dissatisfied with their mate. Sometimes this is legitimate, but often it is because they think the "grass is greener on the other side of the fence." It has been my experience that if in fact the grass is greener, it is because there is more buffalo dung on that side.

Think like a wolf or hawk. Find a mate that wishes to be with you and focus on behavior, not your wishes. Not your wants but behavior. Find someone who wants what you offer.

Know yourself, be true to that knowledge and someone like you will find you. Much like the lightening bugs of a summer evening.

They don't shout, they don't wave, they simply shine their light of truth and anoth-

er fire fly will find them. That is one form of magic.

As men, we should always have the high ground as our goal. In war, make your enemy tire on his way to fight you.

In peace, be above issues and problems that are presented. From the top, you can see further. From the top, you can see the relationship of things below you.

It is always easier to walk the prairie. The ground is flat and you can see for long distances, but there is no shelter.

There are few trees and fewer boulders to increase your vision. In the mountains, travel is more difficult, but there are trees for fire. There are rocks to shelter you from the cold wind. There are streams to drink from and elk to eat.

For most tribes, it is necessary to walk across the prairie in order to hunt in the mountains but, in the mountains, your enemy has more difficulty in sneaking up on you for an ambush. On the prairie, he can be hidden in the grass.

In the mountains, you approach the home of the Great Spirit. On the prairie, you are in the company of man.

Sometimes the high ground means doing the right thing; operating from a position of right, not convenience.

The same is true. The high ground is the path to walk. Do not allow others to move you from that path. It is only by struggle and effort that you come down from the top of a mountain.

Anyone can stand at the bottom and look up. The mountain holds dangers: loose rocks, avalanches and the mighty bear. That is where he goes to sleep his winter sleep.

It is difficult to find a den. It requires much effort, but it is safe—safe from all except man.

The eagle lives in the mountains and flies down to hunt. The eagle builds no nest on the ground for her offspring. Her nests are on rock cliffs or in the tallest trees. They are safe—safe from all except man.

Bob Anderson

Only man, and only some of them, strives to see the next valley from the top of the last hill.

Chapter Nine

These are men you can trust, they are willing to do hard and difficult things.

Honorable men also seek those sights, although they may never climb a mountain to see the valley. These men strive to see the best in other men by demonstrating the best in themselves.

They too do not walk the easy path. Their honor is a heavy weight that requires much effort and can appear to cost them much.

But, as the brave is made stronger by his climb to the top of the mountain, the honorable man is made stronger by the path he has chosen.

There is much danger in the mountains; there is much danger in being honorable. Lesser men will question, "Why do you climb that mountain?" or "Why do you behave so?"

The answer is the same for both and never appreciated by those who have not climbed or those without honor. The an-

swer is, "Because I have seen sights that you cannot imagine."

The brave who climbs to the top of the world understands that as he is standing there looking, looking from the top, the only way he can go is down; but, that is in preparation for the next mountain.

The honorable man, who does right things, knows that he too will only be able to stand at the top of the world for a short time before he takes that next step, which will bring him off the hill.

That too is reasonable because the honorable man knows that the downward stride is taking him to the next point where his honor will be called on.

"But are you saying that we are doomed and our fates are already sealed and there is nothing we can do about our life and our fortunes?"

Not at all. I am simply trying to get you to understand that the stronger the bow, the harder it is to pull. The resistance of the bow becomes its ability to shoot the arrow.

The stronger the bow, the further the arrow will fly. But it is harder to pull. It is heavier to carry. The further you wish the arrow to fly, the stronger the bow must be.

So it is with life. The more you have to work, the more inconvenient it becomes; however, is necessary to attain a lofty goal.

A weak goal is easily attained but where is the joy? What have you learned and how does it improve you? A mighty goal is not easily attained but oh the joy of winning.

As a strong bow strengthens the archer, a mighty goal improves the seeker. That which you wish to do and only requires you to merely accomplish it, can easily be done. The trick is in wanting it "done" enough to work for it.

Mighty goals give mighty victories, just not every time. If you want to shoot the arrow across the canyon, you must make a bow strong enough to throw that arrow across the canyon.

You must make an arrow straight enough to fly across that canyon, and you must practice so that you are strong enough to shoot that arrow accurately.

Also remember: the higher you fly, the further you have to fall. After making the bow, making the arrow and hours upon hours of practice, you fire the arrow and it sails across the canyon.

So what? Probably all you have accomplished is losing the arrow. There was not enough thought given to what the goal was or how much value the goal had.

Do not work hard and long, and practice hard and long, to have a fleeting moment of pleasure that accomplishes nothing except to see the arrow in flight.

Spend your time wisely.

Chapter Ten

The Great Spirit has given each of us a pouch filled with seeds. In those seeds are all of the days we will ever see. You will get no more added to it. Each time you open that pouch to remove that seed, determine what you want to have grown from it.

Should it be an oak that will last a long time? Should it be grain to feed your family? Should it be an herb that can heal? Should it be grass to thatch your home? Should it be a flower whose beauty and smell is for all to enjoy?

The choice is yours and you are free to make it. I would suggest that you stay away from poison ivy, however, it has a lovely flower but it feeds no one.

It will not make wood for a fire. It will not make wood for a bow. It will not make thatch for the room. It serves no purpose except in the sight of the Great Spirit.

Man has no knowledge of its real purpose in His eyes. It simply itches and makes us scratch. While it does feel good *to scratch, it accomplishes nothing except to spread the rash.*

Pick your seeds well. Tend your garden and reap your harvests. But before you pick up the seed, and before you plant your garden, determine what you want to grow.

I took the pipe from him and puffed while I thought. Finally I said, "So you are saying there is no magic. The secret to success is hard work and preparation—not taking the easy path."

Is that not magic? Is not knowledge, magic? If magic is all we do not understand and suddenly we understand, is that not magic? Doing things the easy way is always harder than wishing for it.

It is man's nature, and one of the laws of the Great Spirit, that taking the easy way does not teach man much. By trying to avoid work, more work is created.

Doing things quickly and doing them wrong, means you must do it again. As the white man says, 'There is never enough time to do it right, but there is always time enough to do it over.'

I took a deep puff on the pipe and held the smoke in my lungs for a moment before answering. When I exhaled, I was back in my office at my computer. Grandfather was gone and I was alone again. I began typing and continued to type until the entire visit had been written down.

Chapter Eleven

I lost an entire week of writing following my last visit with Grandfather. It was a week filled with unpleasant surprises and the death of my mother's oldest sister, Eunice.

I have fond memories of Aunt Eunice from my childhood. She was a large woman, most say six feet tall. She had beautiful long auburn hair and I never remember her not laughing.

She had grown up during the Depression and lived for eighty-one years. She had one son and over the last fifteen years had suffered greatly. I understand that she had become difficult and could be hard to get along with. I am glad that I don't have those memories of her.

The other problem that I experienced during that week was the realization that a man I had called my friend for most of my life, was not.

We had experienced difficult times before but I was becoming more and more convinced that this particular impasse would eventually dissolve our friendship.

Almost ten days after my last visit with Grandfather, I sat down to the computer again. I was angry and I was hurt when I began to type. After about an hour of editing and proofing this story, I blinked and I was back in that other place again.

The night was still and clear and the stars sparkled brightly. This time I said simply, "Hello Grandfather."

He said, **Welcome my son. You are troubled, what is the matter?**

"It has been a hard week Grandfather. I have buried my mother's oldest sister and fear I have lost an old friend."

I will say a prayer for your loved one. It is good that she is with the Great Spirit now. Her pain is gone and she is young again.

The pain you feel of her loss is because you do not know how to talk to her. Do not worry; she will speak to you in quiet moments or during the sleeping time. That is when man can listen with his other self and hear what is spoken from the Spirit World. Tell your mother this; it will make her feel better.

On this other matter, we do not lose old friends. Sometimes we misplace them but friends do not go away. Only those who we thought were friends or those we wanted to be our friends, leave.

Man sometimes chooses to fool himself by denying that which is. I knew a man who found a buffalo calf and raised him with cattle. One day, the buffalo tore down all of the man's fences because it could not stand to be pinned in any longer. The buffalo was not doing this out of anger, he was just being a buffalo.

Many times we see creatures that we find beautiful and we try to tame them but they remain what they are by nature. I knew another man who had found a wolf cub whose mother had died. He raised the wolf one day with his dogs but the cub, he was not a dog. The wolf grew to be a big, beautiful animal and played with the man's children and the other dogs.

One day, the wolf became a wolf again. He killed the dogs and attacked the man's son. The man had to shoot the wolf and he cried because he loved the wolf.

In his way the wolf loved the man but the wolf could not change his nature. Eventually, that which made him a wolf, that with which he was born, came alive and he was once again a wolf.

Do you know the story of the young brave and the snake?[2]

I shook my head, no.

Chapter Twelve

One day, long ago a young brave climbed to the top of a mountain to have a vision quest. For three days, he did not sleep and he did not eat.

On the fourth day, the weather became much colder and the brave wrapped himself in his blanket to stay warm.

At this time, a snake crawled up to him. This was still during the time that man and beasts spoke the same language. The snake said, "Young brave, put me in the blanket with you and I will be warm."

The brave said, "You are a snake and you will bite me."

The snake said, "That would not make sense. I need your warmth and it is the kind thing to do. I will not bite you."

The brave saw the reason in this and picked up the snake and placed him in the blanket. The snake squirmed close to the brave and was warmed.

Suddenly, the brave felt fire and realized the snake had bitten him. He threw the snake out and as he lay dying he said, "Why did you bite me? You said you would not and I was trying to help you."

The snake said, "You knew what I was when you placed me there."

The snake was just being true to its nature.

It is easy to see a snake and know there is danger, just as it is easy to see the wolf and know danger.

With man it is harder. Some men have the spirit of good within them, some do not. You cannot tell what spirit is in a man just by listening to him, you can only tell by his behavior.

Once you see how a man behaves, not how he talks, you will know his spirit. You must be close enough to observe the behavior.

Sometimes we get too close and are injured; but, once you know the spirit of a man, you can keep him from hurting you a second time.

Man is a silly creature who believes he is above the laws of the Great Spirit. He is not. He is part of those laws. He is as he is *supposed to be, but he does not understand that his power is not absolute.*

The Great Spirit gave us the buffalo, a monstrous animal. Yet, man can kill him. Man has the bow. Man makes the arrow.

Man sees many things and decides to change them. This is particularly true of the whites. They look at the prairies and see towns. They look at the buffalo and see hats. They look at the Indian and see something lower than themselves.

The white man has what he calls 'technology.' He makes the gun that will shoot further than the strongest bow.

He makes the iron horse to bring more of him to our land. He makes the wires that sing and carry messages from one camp to another across great distance, faster than a bird can fly.

We have never had need of these things because we lived in harmony with the world that the Great Spirit gave us.

Because he can do so much, he believes he can do anything. Because he can change so much in his world, he believes that he can change the world.

Of all of the animals only man can bring forth fire. The problem is that man has forgotten that it was the Great Spirit that gave him fire in the first place.

The Great Spirit makes the law and his laws cannot be broken by man.

Chapter Thirteen

It was months before I saw Grandfather again. I wished I could have spoken with him each day but he was not accessible to my conscious mind. It was as though my dream state sought him and he came.

Then one night I was back and he said, **Come, sit with me. We will make talk, we will make smoke. There is much to learn.**

"What shall we talk about tonight?" I asked.

Let us speak of change. I think you fear change. Why is that?

"I don't know," I said. "I guess I fear change because I don't know what the change will mean. It seems that every time something changes in my life, it is different from what I thought it would be."

He took a puff from the pipe.

"I think the thing will be one thing but it is always something different. Sometimes it is a good change, sometimes it is not. I would like to know how to control it and avoid the bad."

He slowly let out the smoke and waved it up over his face and into his hair. Then he said,

What the caterpillar calls the end, the Great Spirit calls a butterfly.

There comes a time each year when the Great Spirit lays his hands on the world and a terrible and wonderful thing occurs. One beast dies and another is born and they could not be more different.

At the end of its existence, a caterpillar wraps itself inside a blanket and changes. There are struggles and new dangers the creature must face.

There is a legend about a brave who one day found a cocoon with a butterfly trying to be born.[3] The brave decided to help the butterfly. He took out his knife and sliced off the remaining bits of cocoon. The butterfly emerged easily but it had a swollen body and shrivelled wings.

The man brave continued to watch it, expecting that any minute the wings would enlarge and expand enough to support the body.

Neither happened. In fact, the butterfly spent the rest of its life crawling around. It was never able to fly.

What the brave in his kindness and haste did not understand was that the restricting cocoon, and the struggle required by the butterfly to get through the opening, was a way of forcing the fluid from the body into the wings so that it would be ready for flight once that was achieved.

That is nature's way. We are expected—no—we are required to struggle. Sometimes struggles are exactly what we need in our lives. It is how we gain strength.

I said, "In today's world the aspect of immediate gratification, instant communication, instant information—instant just about everything—has become the norm. Unfortunately, we have lost patience. We have lost grace. We have lost dedication to a task or project in the exchange."

"Everything takes longer than it should, it always costs more than we thought and if something can go wrong, it will go wrong and always at the worst possible time."

Truer words are seldom spoken. Very few people I know have had their lives turn out the way they expected.

I nodded. "I know mine sure hasn't. All well laid plans end up being changed by circumstances and situations; by us or by God. Bad decisions hit us like a que ball sending us off spiralling out of control and in directions we never anticipate."

"Yet, I have found that those new directions, as uncomfortable as they are, also sometimes give me benefits that I could not have conceived. I guess the purpose of life is to live it."

"We are supposed to be stretched. We are supposed to be challenged. We are supposed to fail sometimes. The trick is to learn from it."

Unfortunately, some never develop the ability to learn. They keep doing the same thing—the same way—again and again and again and again and again and again and again and again and again and again and again and again and again and again, all the while expecting things to turn out differently.

Chapter Fourteen

"Some people violate what I call the Rule of Ego," I said.

What is that?

With a smile I tried to put it into words he would appreciate, "Never, ever, ever believe your own buffalo dung."

He laughed, *Some folks are simply ignorant of how to do something or how to succeed. I do like ignorant folks though, with just a little education they learn.*

I agreed but added, "Unfortunately, there are some stupid folks. There's nothing you can do with stupid."

He nodded.

I said, "Except do as Bill Engvall suggests and say, 'Here's your sign!'"

Some folks are just their own worst enemy. Some folks get crunched by the universe and wrap themselves in the blanket of victim. It is easier for them to live in the mess they created than to get out of it.

I pondered this and decided this is also something that parents need to remember.

There is a difference between helping and enabling. No parent wants to see their child suffer; yet, it is through that suffering that they grow stronger. It is by working through their problems they find an answer they can own.

Going through life with no obstacles will cripple us. We will not be as strong as we could have been and, like the butterfly, we will never fly.

Chapter Fifteen

"Are you a chief?" I asked.

No, I was once but that was a long time ago. It was a good time but now I am too old and I am just a grandfather.

"What was it like to be a chief?" I asked.

He grew thoughtful. I watched as his eyes looked into his own past and I knew he was seeing himself as he once was; young and strong and a leader.

There is strength in numbers. A single man can kill a single deer. But it takes many warriors to attack a herd of buffalo. In all things, many hands can make the task easier.

In some things, however, many hands can make for confusion if a single mind does not prevail. This is called leadership.

When a wolf hunts alone he must hunt something smaller. It is known by my people that rabbit does not taste as good as elk or the buffalo. When the wolf hunts in a pack, better tasting and larger game can be killed; but, he must share.

So it was with the tribe; we had to share and work together in order to survive and thrive.

The leader of the wolf pack has responsibility for the well-being of the pack. He must locate the food and direct the attack. So it is with man.

The leader must lead but this is not always easy. Like the wolf, a good leader of man must always be the strongest, bravest and smartest. With man it should be so but is not always so.

Man can speak and man can think. Therefore our leaders are sometimes chosen for their ability to speak and their ability to think, not their ability to lead.

When a wolf grows too old to lead the pack, a younger, stronger wolf takes over. Usually this is a battle to the death and the old leader is killed. Man can learn from the wolf but a new leader can learn from an old leader.

It is a fact that the pack survives and flourishes by the actions of each member, not just the leader.

So it is with man. The tribe survives by the actions; the different actions of each member, not just the leader.

Grandfather's face began to change again as he spoke. Suddenly, Crazy Horse, the Cheyenne chief was sitting across from me. Then there was Quanah Parker, the last of the Comanche war chiefs.

The hunters must hunt, the warriors must defend the tribe. The women must do their part and even the children are important. Through them the tribe continues. If the leaders do their part, the children learn from their elders and knowledge increases.

In the world of the wolf and in the world of the man, the leader is responsible for and to those who follow him. The followers are also responsible to the leader.

He morphed again and became Sequoyah, a Cherokee Indian, who according to the *North American Review,* had "requested an educated half-breed, named Charles Hicks, to write his name. In being done, he made a die containing a facsimile of the word, which he stamped upon all the articles fabricated by his mechanical ingenuity.

In the year 1820, while on a visit to some friends in a Cherokee village, he listened to a conversation on the art of writing, which seems always to have been the subject of great curiosity among the Indians.

Sequoyah remarked that he did not regard the art as so very extraordinary, and believed he could invent a plan by which the red man might do the same thing. He persevered in carrying out his intention, and attained his object by forming eighty-six characters.

While thus employed, he incurred the ridicule of his neighbors, and was entreated to desist by his friends. The invention, however, was completely successful and the Cherokee dialect is now a written language."

That leader may lead them through difficult times but the leader knows there is game and water on the other side of this difficulty; and, he is working for them even though they will object.

Sometimes a bad man or a bad wolf will gain leadership. These bad leaders are recognizable because their goals are not the goals of the pack or the tribe. Their goals are their own and they will sacrifice all others to better their position.

Sometimes it is difficult for the pack or the tribe to see this bad leadership. Their job is to follow; but eventually the bad man, or the bad wolf, will be found out and their agenda will be clear to all.

When that happens, it is the nature of the wolf and the nature of the man that the bad leader will be deposed. It is necessary for the health of the pack and the health of the tribe.

Followers must follow but only until it is their time to lead. Not everyone can lead but a leader will emerge.

It is the way of things.

Chapter Sixteen

"What else do I need to know Grandfather?"

For a while he thought, then he said, **Do not spit into the wind. Spitting into the wind is always a mistake. It will come back to you.**

This is also true of doing bad things. The Great Spirit will always arrange for what you've done to come back to you.

Therefore, if all you do is good things, good things will come back to you. If you do bad things, those will come back to you.

This is no great concept, it is reality. Yet we humans continue, by force of will and energy, to attempt to bend the universe to our way of thinking and our own desires.

Some people are actually able to accomplish this to some degree but they fail to realize that the universe is like a bow.

You can bend a strong bow but you cannot hold it in that shape. Either you release the string on purpose and let loose the arrow toward a goal or you will eventually tire and accidentally release it.

Usually this is rather messy; you may get injured but certainly you have accomplished nothing but a lot of noise in the process.

If we cooperate with the universe, we must realize that the universe has its own rules and its own laws.

Anything that we do that is in opposition to those laws may be successful and fulfilling but that success and fulfillment will be short lived; because, like the bow, the universe will return to its normal state, shape and condition.

Chapter Seventeen

"What else, Grandfather?" I asked.

A sharp knife is a safer knife. A dull knife will cut you quicker than a sharp one. Each knife should have a sharp edge that will allow it to be a better knife.

When a knife grows dull, the man must work harder and harder to accomplish the same task.

Working harder with a dull knife does not make the man more successful. The man must be smart enough to realize that he should take time to sharpen the knife. Likewise, the man must realize that he must take the time to sharpen himself.

As with man, it takes time to put the proper edge on a knife. In the old days, it meant selecting a proper piece of flint.

It was necessary to assemble the proper equipment. This included something to shape the flint with and a piece of tough leather to protect your hand as the flint was worked into shape.

Eventually, reshaping of the finished blade was necessary because even flint loses its ability to keep a sharp edge.

When the white man came he brought steel; and, the points for our knives, tomahawks and lances became steel. Steel is easier to sharpen than flint. To sharpen a steel blade you rub it against something that is harder than it is. The same is true of man.

To sharpen a steel blade you must find the correct angle between the blade and the whet rock. Too steep an angle makes a sharp blade, but it is fragile and will dull quickly.

Too shallow an angle makes the blade unsuited for fine work such as skinning and preparing the skin.

We have many tools, though not as many as the white man. We use the knife to cut, the lance to stab and the tomahawk to cut down trees and our enemies.

Each tool takes a different edge and it is also the same with man. Each man must choose his purpose.

A hunter needs a sharp edge that will cut but is light to carry. A warrior needs a blade that is durable and can withstand punishment. A farmer needs a blade that will last for many seasons.

A sharp blade cuts cleanly and accurately. It slices through whatever it is cutting. A dull blade will catch and is difficult to control.

Throughout his discussion, Grandfather's face and appearance continued to change. One moment he was Sitting Bull of the Sioux, the next an Iroquois brave. Then there were a whole series of changes, for each statement there was another face and voice.

An obstacle may throw the blade out of the material it is trying to cut and into the hand, arm or leg of the man using it.

So too it is with a man. A competent man will work through obstacles and can be trusted to accomplish those tasks that are given him.

An incompetent or stupid man is like a dull knife. Once it is removed from the sheath, it is a danger. This man will catch on insignificant thoughts and is difficult to control or work with; and, is a danger to the tribe.

A dull knife can be sharpened. An ignorant man can be trained. Eventually however, the dull knife is no longer capable of being sharpened.

Some men are incapable of being trained.

When the knife is no longer capable of being sharpened and used correctly, discard it. It is dangerous.

When a man in no longer capable of being trained, let that man go off by himself where he is no threat to those around him.

Chapter Eighteen

I asked him, "Grandfather, why do white men live with white men in cities and your people live in their own villages?"

Like attracts like. Wolves run with wolves, the buffalo runs with the buffalo.

Crows do not fly with eagles and the buzzard does not fly with the dove. Therefore, look around you and see whom you are with. It is a mirror of who you are.

The wolf and the hawk mate for life. They seek until they find the one that is like them and then they know this is their partner. Wolves and hawks act; they demonstrate who and what they are.

They dance and they play and through the dances and the playing, they see they are similar.

Man talks and talks and talks. Man can change his face as easily as putting on war paint. Man can lie, animals do not. Man can cheat, animals do not. Man kills for pleasure, animals do not.

Long ago, man and the animals spoke together in one language. We, us and them, lived in the hand of the Great Spirit and then man began to listen to the coyote, the jokester.

Man was seduced by the stories the coyote told him and believed the coyote. Man still does not realize that the call of the coyote is his laughter over the foolishness of man.

Man lies and therefore does not know who he is. How then can he find his partner?

Man shows many different faces and his friends and woman may never know who is the real person. Man, unlike the buffalo, can change his herd.

That is the gift the Great Spirit has given us. We, above all animals, can make choices. We have the power of thought. They have only the power of their instinct.

Chapter Nineteen

The next time I saw Grandfather would also be the last. He was no longer just old, he was older than old. I could see his energy was gone but he still had things to say. I realized that often we forget the wisdom of age and simply see an old person.

I was beginning to realize that behind the wrinkles was still a young man. I could close my eyes and I still see myself young and un-wrinkled.

I knew Grandfather's time was coming.

There are many things I must tell you. My time with you is ending. For now my son, do not speak. You must write as fast as you can.

Doing things that are hard strengthens the person. Man must struggle, that is the way strength is gained.

The Great Spirit places wonderful obstacles in our path so we may exercise our muscles, our heart and our spirit. It is much like climbing the mountain.

It is difficult and many who start do not complete the journey. But only those who have climbed the mountain can appreciate the view.

Man learns best from failure. When man succeeds, he learns very little. Success is to be celebrated, not studied.

Man learns best what not to do by doing it wrong. Man does not have to make all of the mistakes himself.

His face began to change again and again. I knew I was seeing people of every tribe there used to be; warriors, medicine men, chiefs, braves and children of all of the tribes that ever were.

For each statement he made, he changed. For each new thought, there was a different face, different clothing.

Some wore their hair long and free, others wore braids. Some a simple head band. Another wore a Mandan hat. There were war bonnets and single feathers. Some wore a sash of cloth tied around their heads.

Some wore buckskins; others wore the clothing of the white man. Each different.

Some were old, others young. Some wore war paint, others a peaceful serenity. Each new thought brought forth a new face, and the faces spoke more eloquently than the words.

A smart man can learn from the mistakes of others. A smart man can see what someone else did that did not work.

Success is a habit that must be developed. A man must believe that he can be successful before he can become successful. A man must believe that he is worthy of success before he can succeed.

Therefore, small successes are necessary in order for man to learn he is worthy. From many small successes comes the ability to have larger successes. From several larger successes comes the ability to have magnificent successes. Mostly, it is a question of continuing to do right things.

Shooting an arrow into the sky is fun but one often loses the arrow. It is exciting to watch an arrow fly. It is a wonder to watch it climb higher and higher into the sky before it reverses and falls back to the ground. But it is a stupid brave that gam-

bles with the loss of the arrow or the break-ing of the tip.

I would ask, "What did you gain from what you did? Was it worth what it cost you? How many hours of work did you waste for an instant of thrill?"

"Grandfather, where do I fit in?" I asked.

Each feather on a bird is a thing of beauty and a work of the Great Spirit. To see the face of the Great Spirit look at small things, study the feather.

Each feather is a magical thing. Each bird has its own colors and sizes of feather and each feather has its own purpose in being.

Some are for flight, some are for warmth. Each is both a mystery. And now to the question; is there truly a Great Spir-it?

The same question is answered each time there is a birth and each time there is a death. Man could not have made such magic.

Even birds that serve no purpose to man are loved by the Great Spirit. The Great

Spirit created exactly what he knew the world should have.

I do not know the purpose of the ladybug, the fly or the mosquito. But I did not create them. If I had created them, I would know their purpose.

If it exists, it has a purpose. That I do not know its purpose does not change that fact. I must revere all things that exist, because the Great Spirit made them. Just as I have value, so must they.

One day I will understand these things but not today, for I am still a man.

Chapter Twenty

"Sometimes, it seems like there is so much turmoil," I said, as I rubbed my face with frustration. "No matter where I turn, it seems like I'm just spinning out of control."

A quiet walk alone solves many problems. In all things, discussion will show the answer to questions. Sometimes the discussions will be between men. Sometimes it must be between man and the Great Spirit.

The Great Spirit speaks with a quiet voice. Too many distractions will keep a man from hearing it. Being alone with the Great Spirit is the best way to hear him speak—even when He uses no words.

There is a difference between being alone and being lonely. To be alone is not a bad thing. In truth you are not alone, you are with the Great Spirit and He will protect you.

Being lonely, however, is not a good thing. Man can be lonely within his tribe. Man can be lonely in the midst of many.

Man will be lonely when his heart is filled with trouble and grief. Man will be lonely when his heart is filled with anger and hate. Man will be lonely when he loses faith.

Once he has decided to walk again with the Great Spirit, he will appear to be alone to other men, for they cannot see the Great Spirit with him. They can only see when the Great Spirit is in him.

Chapter Twenty-One

I didn't know what I could believe in. Yet, I saw Grandfather did. He knew what he could believe in and part of what he believed in was me; more accurately—what I could become.

Hidden behind each cloud is a mystery that will be solved when someone sees behind the cloud. There are many mysteries in this world but each mystery has a solution.

The problem is we have not discovered what the solution is. That does not detract from its existence.

As the cloud may hide the mountaintop, it does not mean the mountaintop does not exist. The Great Spirit has already answered all questions. This is reality. He is the strongest Grandfather.

We do not know all of the answers. This also is reality and it is the purpose for man's existence, to learn.

Perhaps we need to climb higher to see the top of the mountain. Of course we can see the mountaintop on a sunny day from the valley. But the view is much different from the top.

There are no answers in this world, only interesting questions. Grandfather has said that the Great Spirit has already answered all questions. How then can he now say there are no answers in this world, only interesting questions?

It is simple, Grandfather is old and he is wise. He realizes that for each question, there are as many answers as there are men to ask the question. For each man, there may be a different yet equally correct answer.

Lastly, each time a single man asks a question, he may find a different answer, because he himself is different from the last time he asked the question.

Life is like the swirl of the campfire. It constantly changes as it consumes the wood.

Likewise, life changes as it consumes the man.

Chapter Twenty-Two

I asked him about how—no—why life was so hard.

He said, *Life is not hard, you are too soft.*

Can you shoot your own dog? A dog is a wonderful companion. He warns us of danger and he makes us laugh. He works beside us and he plays with the child.

The question is not, "Do you want to shoot your own dog?" The question is, "If it became necessary to shoot your dog, because the dog was sick or hurt or dying, would you be strong enough to do the hard thing? Or would you let someone else be responsible for doing what you should do?"

Dogs are a wonderful gift of the Great Spirit but with each gift comes responsibility—the price for the use of those gifts. We are ultimately responsible for those things in our life.

The job of a parent is not to help the child become a good person; it is to make that child a good enough person to make the grandchild a good person. Each man stands on the shoulders of the man that came before him.

Each man is responsible for the person that will follow.

Our greatest responsibility is not to prepare our children to be good adults—strong and brave. Our greatest responsibility is to prepare them to teach our grandchildren to be good adults—strong and brave.

Do not mourn for the dead, grieve for the living.

Each of us will come to the end of our trail in our own time—some sooner, some later. Each will happen at the time it should happen.

When a person dies they should not be mourned, for they have moved to a different place with the Great Spirit. Their journey has been completed.

It is for the living we should shed a tear. We miss the one departed. We have memories that cause us pain; we have an emptiness. That is because something and someone we value has gone from our world.

The departed has no such emptiness. By walking with the Great Spirit, the departed realizes the answers to all questions. The departed sees all things as they truly are.

He has no longing for the world he left behind because he knows it is not left behind. It is a part of all things and this is simply the way of things. It is only the living who do not understand.

Life is hard. From the moment of the first breath, man must struggle. He must struggle against the elements. He struggles against his nature. He struggles against other men.

It is in this struggle that he becomes strong and productive. By struggling, he puts meaning to his existence. By struggling, he shows his children the ways of the world and what victory and defeat look like.

Chapter Twenty-Three

I thought he was taking me down the path where I would need to start making my dreams come true. I was wrong again.

The Great Spirit has said, "What is—is; therefore, what is not—is not." There are many things in the world that appear to be one thing but in fact are another. Man can be confused by appearances.

The Great Spirit is not, for he has created all that is. As there is day, there is night. As there is hot, there is cold. As there is good, there is evil.

Many of man's problems are not from seeing what is but from failing to see what is not.

Be not sad that it is over—rejoice that it occurred. Man is the only greedy animal. While the squirrel stores nuts for the winter, man stores nuts just to have them.

When man experiences joy, he fears the passing of the joy. Therefore, for man, there is an emptiness that no other creature feels.

For man there is a beginning and an end. For all other animals there is only the now.

Because man understands that death will come to all people, he also understands that pleasure is transient, wonder is temporary and love can die as easily as man.

The Great Spirit knows and speaks the answers to all questions. Man does not listen well. The Great Spirit loves man above all else that he has created.

The Mother Earth and the Father Sun were created to feed and care for man. But man is also like the chattering squirrel. He barks at the wind and does not listen to the sounds of the forest.

If man could be still, he could hear the answers to all of his questions. But that is not the nature of man.

Because you are the only voice in the forest does not mean you are wrong. There is truth in the nature of things.

Although a fish does not feel water, that does not mean he is not wet. Though a worm does not feel the earth, it does not mean he is not dirty.

Sometimes a man will see a truth that his brothers do not. That his brothers do not see does not change the reality. Just as a mountain is hidden by a cloud, truth can be hidden from one who does not see.

The mountain is still there, even if it cannot be seen. So then is the truth still there.

Chapter Twenty-Four

I began seeing that his guidance was something I had already been following. I just didn't know it. I hadn't ever put it into words.

A lightening bug does not call his brothers. He simply shines his own light and they will come to him. When the snows have gone and the forest is green again, the lightening bug comes.

He has no voice to call his brothers. He has only a light. But by shining his light, he is able to show where he is and others like him find their way to him.

So it is with good people. They do not shout; they simply shine their light and other good people find them.

On the long road, the hard way is most often the easiest and the shortest. In the struggle that man must endure, it is the challenges of winning that prepare him for the next struggle.

Therefore, the smart man embraces the challenges of life because within each challenge is a reward. With each victory comes knowledge and strength.

That is the way of the world. A warrior that always picks the easy path will only see what others have seen. The warrior that climbs the mountain will know the view that few have seen.

The shortest way between two places is best shared by friends. A friend is a drink of cool water on a hot day. A friend is comfort in a troubled world. A friend knows us for what we are and loves us anyway. A friend keeps us from believing our own lies.

Why have people in your life that hurt your heart? Let them walk their way and you walk your way, but walk in different ways.

There are people that will be drawn to you because of your strength. Some of them will be as strong as you are. With these people, walking the trails of the forest is an exciting and wonderful thing. Each day is an adventure and both give to the other.

Some of the people are drawn to you because they need your strength. They want to be taken care of; they want you to take care of them.

These people will not give you anything—they take. You cannot fix them. If they could be fixed, they would already be fixed. This does not make them bad people but they are bad for you.

Chapter Twenty-Five

"Why is it that some folks seem so right but it turns out so wrong?" I asked.

Fire burns and water cools. But fire can light the darkness and water can flood a village—it is all in the way it is applied.

Within each element there is both positive and negative. It is the way of things. Man's dilemma is to determine how to use the positive and avoid the negative.

War is an ugly thing but not the ugliest of things. War is in the nature of man. It, like all else, has been created by the Great Spirit for a purpose.

While war should not be sought, man has not learned how to do without it. War serves a purpose but man should never serve war.

To be brave does not mean to have no fear. Bravery is being afraid and still going on.

Bravery means acting against one's nature because it is the right thing to do.

Bravery means a willingness to sacrifice one's self for his brothers, for the village.

Bravery is expensive. It is not easy. But it is easier than being a coward. A brave man is too much of a coward to be called a coward.

Chapter Twenty-Six

"But I can't seem to get them to change," I said, frustrated. "It seems so obvious why what they are doing is wrong!"

Let each man chose his own way. Let each man walk his own path. It is not right or appropriate to force someone to your will.

It is a small thing. No one knows how to tell another man to live his life. Each of us is the total of all we know, all we question, all we have won and all we have lost.

It is inappropriate and impolite to tell another what to do. It is not the way of the people.

It is a greater thing to touch an enemy than to kill him. To kill an enemy is a great thing. But it is greater to vanquish without killing. This allows for families to stay together. It keeps blood feuds from continuing.

It is far braver to approach an enemy and touch him than it is to stand off and simply kill him.

Always bathe below the village. Always water the horses below the village. A man should not bathe in the river above the village.

A man should keep his horses also from that place. Water can be fouled by man or beasts and the village should not have to drink that water.

Honor our Mother, the earth. She will take care of her children. The Earth is our mother. She gave us food and the buffalo for all things. She will care for us always. We must care for her. We must love her and honor her as all children should love and honor their mother.

All things that can be thought, have been thought, I think. Since the first man and the first woman came together and gave birth to the people, man has been thinking, dreaming and working.

By now it has all been said. All we do now is to repackage what has been said and done before us. That is all that is new, the wrapping paper of the present.

Never pet a barking dog. A barking dog does not listen to you. For some reason, he

is agitated by your approach. Understand—
he will bite you.

Be aware of that fact. The dog cannot
help the outcome of your encounter; he is
simply following the nature of himself.
You, on the other hand, can change what
will happen.

Chapter Twenty-Seven

"Why is it so hard to deal with women?" I asked; not expecting the answer I received.

Some women have little snakes in their head. Some women have big snakes in their head. All women have snakes in their heads. Men and women do not think alike. This is a basic truth.

Because of the differences between man and woman, it is easy to attack and criticize the other. While it may be relevant, it is never a good idea because it will change nothing.

Trying to make the other change is like trying to teach a bull to sing. It does not work and it makes the bull mad.

There are some things that should be said for the saying. There are some things that should be said for the hearing. There are some things that should not be said at all. Man's greatest challenge is figuring out which is which.

Hawks, like wolves, mate for life. When man has found the right woman, his life is changed.

As you see a hawk and then his mate, as you see the wolf and then his mate, so do you see the man and then his mate. Should his woman die, you see only half as much.

When Grandfather stopped speaking, his face returned to the one I knew and had grown to love. He smiled and took a long drag on the pipe and slowly let out the smoke.

He waved it over my face and up over my head ... and he slowly faded away as did the smoke.

Like the smoke which fades from view but lingers as a fragrance, Grandfather's essence has stayed with me all of these years.

I had been blessed.

Epilogue

There are times, even today, when I almost see Grandfather out of the corner of my eye. Sometimes, it is something on a breeze that smells like his smoke.

Sometimes it is the wind moving through the trees that almost sounds like his laughter. But it has been a long time since we sat and talked and made smoke.

I can almost hear him saying, **There is still much to learn. There was a white man named Mignon McLaughlin who said, 'Even cowards can endure hardship; only the brave can endure suspense.'**

Be brave.

Acknowledgments

There are many people that have come into my life at interesting times to teach me something and then to leave. Sometimes I was glad to see them come.

Sometimes I was glad to see them go. Sometimes I was really glad; but when some left, they took a part of me. In that taking, they left part of themselves. That part lives in a special place within my heart and memories.

Many are people I met in the military and as is the usual case in the military, we have moved on and lost touch with each other. Hopefully this book will draw us back together.

Many are civilians. Luckily most are still alive but, like leaves on a tree, we have been scattered by the winds of time. To all of you I say "Wa Do," that is Cherokee for thank you. Thank you for having touched my life. Thank you for the teachings you gave me.

The Cheyenne tribe had a warrior society called the Dog Men, also known as Dog Soldiers. Each member of the Dog Men wore on his chest a whistle made of the bone of a bird.

Four of the bravest Dog Men were chosen to wear sashes of tanned skins called "dog ropes" or "leashes" into battle.

Attached to each dog rope was a picket-pin (used to tether horses). The pin was driven into the ground as a mark of resolve in combat. When a Dog Man was staked to the ground in order to cover the retreat of his companions, he was required to remain there even if death was the consequence.

The Dog Man could pull the pin from the ground only if his companions reached safety or another Dog Man released him from his duty. The ritual signified that there was no surrender, simply victory or death. You weren't able to retreat and that was your chunk of land.

N. Scott Momaday wrote of them, *"The dog soldiers were the elite military organizations in the tribe. They were the last line of defense for the people. And so they were greatly esteemed. The warriors in the society were outfitted with a particular sash, which trailed the ground.*

And each member carried a sacred arrow. And in time of battle, the dog soldier would impale the sash to the ground and stand the ground to the death. They had a song which only the members could sing, and only in the face of death.

So you can imagine, that children, when they saw a dog soldier go by, must have just said— Ahhh, wow! Look at that guy, he's a dog sol-dier!"

Everyone knew that the Dog Man could be counted on to take a stand and fight to the finish. He was a leader because he was a serv-ant.

Notes

1. The Story of the Peace Pipe: A Sioux Legend, author unknown, public domain information.

2. The Story of Young Brave and the Snake, author unknown, public domain information.

3. The Struggling Butterfly Story, author unknown, public domain information.

Peace Pipe
by Bob Anderson

This pipe was hand made by the author, Bob Anderson, with approximately 360 hours of work with hand files (jewelers), a coping saw and hand drills.

The stem was made from a single piece of wood that was drilled from both ends until a passage was created.   The pipe stone was purchased from the last quarry of its type.

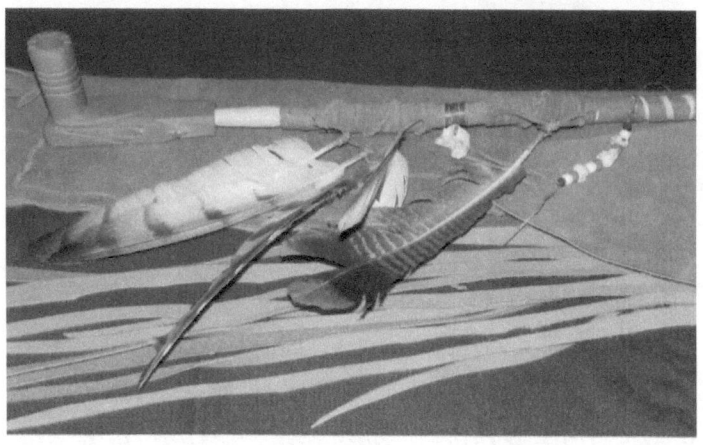

Eagle Cover Photo

Cover Photo of the eagle taken by Paul Gregg on March 23, 2012. Paul has this to say:

The exact location is a fairly well guarded secret due to the fact the Bald Eagle's nest is within the city limits of Houston, Texas. The mated pair of bald eagles have nested there and raised young for a few years now and this year had one eaglet.

When this photo was taken, the adults were kept busy feeding the eaglet that was almost as large as they are. I count it a high privilege when photographing these regal birds.

They are making a great comeback from once being on the endangered species list, to a protected list. There are a number of bald eagle pairs within a 50 mile radius of Houston. Sometimes to exit the area where I have been photographing them, I have to walk directly under one tree where the adults sometimes perch. Looking down on me, they seem to know I'm not there to hurt them, but to highly regard them and share my adoration of them.

Bald Eagles are nesting inside the city limits of Houston, Texas. Their comeback across the country is phenomenal. May their comeback be inspiration for our own return to adherence to our U.S. Constitution!

Bob is a speaker and avid writer. As a speaker, his power message advocates doing hard things, especially when it's unpopular or uncomfortable to do so; simple and back to basics. He believes in unwavering commitment and courage. He believes success is earned, not given; it's a privilege, not a right.

Bob retired as a Chief Master Sergeant from the United States Air Force Reserve (USAFR) with over 32 years of service.

He is co-author of **The Survivalist** series with Jerry and Sharon Ahern (starting with book #30). Additionally, he's the author of **TAC Leader-What Honor Requires**, **Sarge, What Now?**, **Grandfather Speaks** and **Anderson's Rules**.

Bob is a qualified rappel master, holds a 2nd degree black belt in karate, and is an expert in weaponry and military tactics. He and his wife Pamela reside in Missouri.

www.BobAndersonBooks.com

Presentations
by Bob Anderson

Excellence Ain't Easy!
(Motivation/Personal Development)

Can You Shoot Your Own Dog?
(Leadership)

You Can't See-saw By Yourself!
(Teamwork)

Say What?
(Improved Communications)

Everything and More!
(Motivation/Personal Development)

To inquire about having Bob speak at your next event, please visit **www.BobAndersonBooks.com**